The
Rescued
Puppy

The Rescued Puppy

by Holly Webb
Illustrated by Sophy Williams

tiger tales

For Ethan and Harry

tiger tales

5 River Road, Suite 128, Wilton, CT 06897
Published in the United States 2017
Originally published in Great Britain 2011
by Little Tiger Press
Text copyright © 2011 Holly Webb
Illustrations copyright © 2011 Sophy Williams
Author photograph copyright © Nigel Bird
My Naughty Little Puppy illustration copyright © Kate Pankhurst
ISBN-13: 978-1-68010-402-8
ISBN-10: 1-68010-402-0
Printed in China
STP/1000/0236/0918

10 9 8 7 6 5 4 3

For more insight and activities, visit us at www.tigertalesbooks.com

Chapter One

"I still think the blue leash was better," Alex said, staring down at Cooper's new leash with his arms folded and a sulky expression on his face.

"No, red looks great with his fur. If you hadn't spent all your money on candy, you could have bought the new leash!" Becky pointed out. "This is Cooper's first walk. Do you want

Mom to say we can't go because we're fighting? She will, you know!"

"Oh, all right...," Alex muttered. Then he grinned at his twin sister. "I don't think you're going to be able to get the leash on him, anyway!"

Cooper, Becky and Alex's cocker spaniel puppy, was dancing around Becky's feet, squeaking and yipping with excitement.

"Cooper, hold still!" Becky giggled, trying to hook the leash onto his collar. "Look, we won't ever get to take a walk if you won't let me clip this on!"

"Are you two ready yet?" Mom came into the hallway. "Where are we going for this special walk?"

"The park!"

"The woods!"

Becky and Alex spoke at the same time, and Mom sighed. "I think Alex's probably got the better idea this time, Becks. The woods might be too tiring for Cooper on his first big walk. The paths are so narrow, and Cooper would be scrambling over fallen trees and things. Let's get him used to something easier first."

Becky sighed. "I guess. I bet he'll love the woods when he's bigger, though. Oooh!" Quickly she clipped the leash onto Cooper's collar, while the puppy was distracted, looking at Mom. "There! Now we're ready!"

Cooper pulled excitedly at the new leash, twirling himself around Becky's ankles. He had been on a leash before, for his trips to the vet and the puppy parties he'd been to in order to get used to other dogs, but it was still very exciting. He could feel that Becky and Alex were excited about something, too, and he couldn't stop jumping up and down.

Alex and Becky had gotten Cooper two months before, as a joint ninth birthday present. They had been trying

for a while to persuade their parents to get a dog, but Mom and Dad had only just decided that they were old enough. Luckily, Becky and Alex had agreed that they would really love a spaniel— one of their friends at school, Max, had a beautiful black cocker spaniel named Jet, and they both loved to play with him when Max's mom brought him to pick up Max after school.

Becky and Alex's mom had asked where Jet had come from, and Max's mom had given her the name of the cocker spaniel breeder. She told them the puppies were all very well taken care of and used to children. But when Becky and Alex's mom called, there was only one 10-week-old puppy left, and no new litter was expected for a while.

So the whole family had driven over to see him right away.

At first, all they could see was the puppy's mom, lying on a fluffy blanket. She was the most beautiful golden and white spaniel, with the longest, silkiest ears they'd ever seen.

"Oh, wow…," Becky breathed. "Can we pet her?"

Laura, the breeder, nodded. "Just gently, though. You have to be careful with mother dogs when they have their puppies with them."

Alex frowned. "But she doesn't— I can't see a puppy!"

Becky grabbed his hand. "Look!" she said in an excited whisper. "I just saw him—he's fast asleep, snuggled up right next to her. He's beautiful!"

Alex leaned over. "I thought that was his mom's tail," he admitted. "He's really cute. And tiny!"

Laura laughed. "You should have seen him when he was born. He isn't really that small; to be honest, I think his mom is sitting on him."

Becky knelt down to get a closer look. "Yes, she is. Doesn't he mind?"

"No, he's all warm and cozy. He likes being the only puppy left— it means he gets all the attention, from his mom and us. He's going to want a lot of cuddles if you take him home."

Alex and Becky exchanged grins. That sounded perfect.

Just then, the little dog sighed, yawned, and opened his eyes. He looked at his mother and wriggled his bottom indignantly to tell her to get off of him. Then he heaved himself up and looked around, his tail wagging shyly. Who were all these people staring at him?

"Oh, he's so beautiful...," Becky whispered, then turned to her mom and dad. "Look at him! Isn't he perfect?"

He really was like a perfect mini

version of his mom, curly ears and all. He was golden and white, with white patches on his back and a scatter of sweet brownish-gold spots around his shiny black nose. His eyes were almost black, too, and very bright and curious-looking, topped off with long whiskery eyebrows that made him look like a little old man.

Everyone had agreed that he was the perfect puppy, and Laura had said that they could come back and take him home the very next day. It was a few weeks before Becky and Alex's birthday, but they didn't mind having their present early. As Becky pointed out the next day, as they carefully carried the puppy out of Laura's house to put him into the new pet carrier in

the back of the car, they were lucky to have him at all. If they had waited any longer, there might not have been any puppies left.

"And he's lucky to have us, too," Alex said. "I bet he wouldn't have liked anybody else as much. Oof!" He laughed, and wiped off a smear of dog drool, as the puppy gave him a wet kiss across his chin.

Soon Alex and Becky couldn't imagine not having Cooper. He was very friendly, and played endless games of chase and fetch with them in the yard. He loved running so much that he'd bound up and down, and then just suddenly flop down on the grass and fall asleep, absolutely worn out. Becky called it his "off button"; it made her burst out laughing every time.

But although Cooper loved running around in the yard, Alex and Becky had learned that cocker spaniels shouldn't really go for walks until they are about four or five months old. Alex had read it in the book they'd bought, and on a special cocker spaniel website. Becky hadn't believed him at first.

"Why not?" she'd demanded.

Alex had shrugged. "It says they love long walks when they're older—lots of long walks—but you shouldn't wear them out too much when they're little. Just exercise in the yard."

Now that they had Cooper, Becky could understand why both the website and the book had suggested it. Cooper was still quite a small dog, but he was getting heavy. If they'd gone on a long walk and he'd switched off like he did when they were playing, he'd be a real armful to carry all the way home. But now that he was almost five months old, he wasn't getting quite as tired, and Mom and Dad agreed that he was ready for a real walk, just as long as they were careful not to go too far.

Luckily, the park was close enough

that they'd be able to carry the puppy home if he did get really worn out.

Alex opened the front door, and Cooper sniffed the air outside. The front yard smelled different than the back—more cars, and there was definitely a cat hanging around somewhere. He looked up at Becky hopefully. Were they going out?

She laughed at his eager little face. "Come on!"

Alex ran down the path to open the gate, and Cooper gave an excited squeak.

"Try and remember not to let him pull!" Mom called, as she locked the front door and hurried after them. Becky and Alex had started bringing Cooper to puppy obedience classes soon

after they brought him home. They'd spent a lot of time working on walking to heel, but Cooper was so excited at going somewhere new that there wasn't much chance of him doing that now.

"Oh, yes." Becky quickly grabbed a dog treat out of her pocket and held it in front of Cooper's nose, moving it back so that he was standing by the side of her leg, just as she'd practiced in the puppy obedience classes. Then she walked on down the path, and gave Cooper the treat as he trotted nicely alongside her.

"We can run with him in the park, though, can't we?" Alex asked Mom. "I don't mean we'll let him off the leash; I know he's not old enough for that. But can we run fast with him?"

"Of course you can!" Mom smiled. "It's just best to try and keep him calm on the way there. We can't expect Cooper to be perfect, though; it's all so different from our yard at home."

But Cooper had stopped wanting to dance around, anyway. He was much too busy for that. When he'd gone out for rides in the car before, to puppy

training and visits to see friends, he'd always been carried. There was so much more to see down at nose level now! To see and thoroughly sniff.

Becky giggled as they stopped at the seventh lamppost—still on their road. "You know, if we want to be back by dinnertime, I'm not sure we're going to make it to the park!"

Chapter Two

They only made it just inside the park gates on that first walk before Cooper started to drag on his leash and look up hopefully to be carried. Becky and Alex took turns carrying the weary puppy home.

But over the next few weeks, a short walk every day soon stretched into two short walks, and then a quick run

around the houses before breakfast and a longer walk after school, in the park or the woods. By the time Becky and Alex left school for summer vacation, walks were Cooper's absolute favorite thing.

They celebrated the beginning of vacation by taking a picnic lunch with them to the woods. It was a beautiful, hot day, perfect for a long expedition. Mom took a lawn chair so she could sit down with a book while Becky, Alex, and Cooper raced around the woods, shouting and calling and playing hide-and-seek among the tree roots.

Cooper adored the woods. They were full of amazing smells, good places to dig, and sticks that Becky and Alex could throw for him to chase. He had an extending leash now, as no one was sure

about letting him run free just yet. But the absolute best thing about the woods was that they were full of squirrels. Cooper adored squirrels. They were fast, and they smelled interesting, and they bounced up and down when they scampered along. He was desperate to catch one. He'd never gotten anywhere near, but he wasn't giving up hope. And there was a squirrel now....

Alex raced behind Cooper, laughing as the puppy pulled the leash out to its full length and galloped down the path, ears flapping as if he were about to take off. The squirrel was a plump, bushy-tailed one, and it wasn't scared. It seemed to keep looking back to see how close the puppy was getting.

"Alex!" Becky yelled worriedly.

"Don't let him catch it! He'll hurt it! Or it might scratch him!"

But Alex was too far away to hear—or he just wasn't listening, Becky thought angrily as she dashed after them. She really didn't want Cooper to hurt the squirrel.

But when she caught up with Alex and Cooper, she saw that she had worried for nothing. Alex was leaning against a tree, panting, and Cooper was jumping up and down and scratching at the trunk, whimpering.

The squirrel was sitting on a branch halfway up, squeaking and chittering as though it were scolding Cooper.

"Didn't you hear me yelling?" Becky demanded. "What do you think he'd do if he caught it?"

Alex shook his head and shrugged. "No idea! I don't think he knows, either. Calm down, Becky! He's never going to get one."

Cooper ignored them, staring hopefully up at the squirrel as it danced up and down on its branch. Unfortunately, it didn't look as though it were going to fall off.

By the time they trailed back to the clearing where Mom was sitting, they were all really hungry. They had brought Cooper's dog biscuits with them, and a bottle of water and his bowl so he could have a picnic, too. He wolfed down the biscuits in about two seconds, and then stood staring at Alex's tuna sandwiches as if he were starving.

Becky giggled. "You should learn to like egg salad, Alex. He never wants my sandwiches."

Alex shuddered. "Yuck."

Mom slipped her cardigan off her shoulders, enjoying the sun. "Just think, this time next week we'll be on vacation in Seaside, California!"

Becky opened her chips and sneakily fed a very small one to Cooper. He wasn't really supposed to have them, but she couldn't resist those big, hopeful dark eyes.

"We've never been on vacation with a dog before," Alex said happily, stretching himself out on the blanket.

"It's right by the ocean, isn't it?" Becky asked again. She already knew it was—she'd seen the photos in the

vacation cottage brochure—but she liked to hear her mom say it.

Mom smiled at her. "Right next to it, Becks. A little cottage just at the top of a cliff."

"And we'll be allowed to take Cooper for walks, all by ourselves?" Alex pushed himself up on his elbows.

"As long as you're very, very careful and sensible." Mom and Dad had discussed this with them when they'd first booked the cottage. It was in a conservation area, where there were no roads—just a little track that led up to the cottage.

Alex and Becky nodded. They would be super-careful. They lived in a busy town, close to a main road that they had to cross in order to get anywhere,

so Mom and Dad weren't happy about letting them take Cooper out on their own at home. That was why they had looked for a vacation home situated in a quiet place. Beachview Cottage wasn't far from a pretty seaside town called Salt Point, but it was all on its own on a cliff, surrounded by footpaths. It was going to be wonderful.

"I'm going to start packing when we get home," Becky said dreamily. "We'll have to remember to pack all of Cooper's things, too. I wonder if there's a pet store in Salt Point."

Alex smirked. "So you can buy him another fancy collar?" Then he rolled out of the way as Becky aimed a smack at him.

Cooper gave a little warning bark.

He didn't like it when they argued. He didn't understand that they were just teasing each other, even though Becky had tried telling him it was just what twins did. It seemed to Cooper that they were really angry with each other. He looked from Becky to Alex and back again, his eyes worried, and whined sadly.

"Sorry, Cooper." Becky wriggled over to him, and rubbed his ears and scratched his silky spaniel forehead. "It's okay. We were just playing."

Cooper flopped down, head on paws, with a small sigh of relief. His eyes were closing, and within seconds he was asleep in the sun.

Chapter Three

"I wish Cooper could come in the back seat with us," said Becky, as she gently placed the puppy in his travel crate in the back of the SUV. She caught Dad's eye and sighed. "Oh, it's all right, Dad. I know he can't. But it's just such a long trip! He's going to be miserable stuck in that crate. And it would be so nice to have him to cuddle on the way."

Dad shook his head. "Until he starts jumping around and being silly, and distracting me and Mom when we're driving. Don't worry. We'll stop at a rest area when we're halfway there, and we'll get Cooper out and you can take him to stretch his legs. He'll probably go to sleep, now that we've put his favorite blanket in the crate for him."

"I hope so," Becky said, patting Cooper gently and rubbing his ears before she closed the door of the crate. "See you soon, sweetheart."

"You get in, Becky. I'll go and see what's keeping your mom and Alex."

But Alex was already stomping down the path, lugging his backpack and looking grumpy. Mom followed along behind, shaking her head.

"He'd repacked everything!" she told Dad. "And taken out half the clothes! It's a good thing I checked. He had a skateboard in there instead!"

Dad blinked. "But I packed his skateboard—it's next to Cooper's travel crate. I'm sure I put it there."

Mom rolled her eyes. "Apparently he needs two."

"Wow. Oh, wow…," Becky breathed. She was standing in front of the cottage, with Cooper in her arms, staring out at the sea. He hadn't minded the car ride that much—he'd slept most of the time, like she had hoped. But he was definitely glad to be out of his crate.

They'd just arrived, and Becky and Alex had burst out of the car with Cooper to take a look around.

"It's beautiful," Becky whispered.

The sun was shining, and it had turned the water to silver, as though a sparkling pathway was stretched across the sea, calling them down to the beach.

"It really is right next to the sea," Alex said, grinning. He turned around to look at the cottage behind them, a small, white building, very low to the ground, as if it were trying to hide from the winds that swept across the cliff top. "And there's the path down to the beach —look!" He pointed to a little path, half natural, but with steps carved into it here and there to make the steep descent to the sand easier.

"Can we go down…?" Becky started to say, but Mom was waving to them.

"Come and help unpack. It won't take long, and then we can all head to the beach."

Becky sighed and headed back to the car to get her backpack. Cooper made a little whining noise, twisting in her arms to look at the glittering water. He wanted to go closer. He'd never seen anything like it before. Becky hugged him tightly. "I know, Cooper. I want to go and play down there, too. Soon, I promise."

She dashed inside, chasing after Alex, who was already stomping up the stairs. He flung open the bedroom door that Mom had pointed out and yelled, "I get the top bunk!"

"Hey, no fair!" Becky moaned from the doorway. Cooper wriggled out of her arms and went to explore. "Why do you get the top one? Can't we switch halfway through the vacation?"

Alex climbed up the ladder to throw his bag on the bed and stared down at her smugly. "Nope. I called it. Sorry, Becks."

Becky stamped her foot angrily, and Cooper, who was sniffing around under the bunk bed, backed further underneath it, tucking his tail between his legs. They were fighting again. He hated it when they did that. Quietly, he sneaked along under the bed, heading for the bedroom door. Then he bolted out as Becky snapped at Alex, and stood shivering on the landing. He wanted to get away from the loud, scary voices.

Becky and Alex's mom had been looking around, checking out the different rooms and starting to put things away. She'd opened the door of the large cupboard at the top of the stairs, thinking to herself how useful it would be for hanging wet beach towels. Then she'd closed it again,

but she didn't see that it had swung open a little as she walked away, and now Cooper nosed his way inside. It was warm and dark and safe next to the hot water tank, and no one was shouting in here. He curled up on an old towel that the last family must have left behind, and waited for his heart to stop thumping anxiously.

Back in the bedroom, Becky suddenly stopped arguing, and smiled as a thought occurred to her. "All right. You can have the top bunk. I don't mind."

"What?" Alex glared at her suspiciously. "For the entire vacation?"

Becky smiled even wider. "Yes. The entire vacation."

Alex nodded slowly. "Okay."

Becky sat down on the bottom bunk and patted it happily. "Cooper won't be able to get up the ladder, you know. So I get him on my bed for the entire time."

At home Cooper slept on either Becky's bed or Alex's, depending on how he felt. Sometimes he switched beds in the middle of the night, but he was usually curled up on Becky's toes when she woke up in the morning.

Alex scowled. "Hey, that's not fair...."

"You wanted the top bunk," Becky sang triumphantly. "Now you've got it!"

Alex slumped down next to her. "Humph. Cheater!"

"Nope, just more clever than you. Hey, where is Cooper?" Becky sat up, looking around worriedly. "He was

exploring a minute ago. Oh, no—he hates when we fight."

Alex jumped up from the bed. "What if he ran outside? He doesn't have a clue where he's going around here."

They raced out of the bedroom, calling worriedly. "Cooper! Here, Cooper! Where are you, boy?"

"Did you lose him?" Mom popped her head out of her bedroom, looking anxious. "Oh, you two! I heard you fighting. Did you upset him?"

Dad came up the stairs. "I've been unloading the car and I haven't seen him come out the door. He must be in the cottage somewhere. Both of you really need to behave better around him. It's part of being proper dog owners—you

40

have to be careful not to frighten your puppy."

"Sorry, Dad," Alex and Becky muttered, both looking guilty.

"He couldn't have gone far," said Dad. "Come on. I'll check downstairs and you two take another look up here."

"Maybe he's under the bed!" Alex dashed back into their room.

Becky looked along the landing, wondering where she would hide if she were a frightened little puppy. Somewhere dark and cozy, probably. Under the bed was a good idea …. Then she spotted the cupboard door, still slightly open, and padded quietly over to it. She swung the door open gently and crouched down to peer inside.

Cooper stared back at Becky, his eyes round and watchful, and thumped his tail slowly on the towel.

"Hey, Cooper…," Becky whispered sadly, looking at his worried little face. "We scared you, didn't we? Come on out, sweetie. We won't fight anymore."

Alex appeared behind her, and Becky glanced up warningly, her finger to her lips. Alex nodded. "It's okay, Cooper," he whispered. "We'll be nice."

Cooper stood up and nosed at Becky's hands lovingly. She picked him up, and Alex petted his ears gently.

"I'm really sorry, Cooper. Alex, we can't fight while we're here, okay?"

Becky looked at him seriously. "Or we have to try not to, anyway. We can't risk upsetting Cooper and having him run off in a strange place."

Alex nodded. "Vacation truce." He grinned. "Mom and Dad will be happy. Their quietest vacation ever!"

After the world's speediest lunch— Alex and Becky both claimed they weren't hungry, but Mom didn't believe them—they finally got to go down to the beach to explore with Cooper. It was amazing. Because the beach wasn't really close to the town, there was hardly anybody there—just one family building a sand castle, and

a group of older boys swimming at one end.

"There's a bigger beach just a little further along the coast down at Salt Point, with an ice-cream shop and a pier," Mom explained. "But you aren't allowed to take dogs onto Salt Point Beach in the summer."

"I don't mind." Becky gazed at the brown sand, which was striped with pebbles and framed by the tall, reddish-brown cliffs. "It's beautiful here. Just us and the ocean. Do you think we could let Cooper off the leash? He'd have to go all the way back up the path to get lost."

Dad nodded. "As long as we keep an eye on him."

Cooper barked excitedly as Becky

unclipped his leash. He wasn't used to being allowed to run off wherever he liked, and at first he simply raced up and down the sand, barking and jumping and chasing his tail.

Then he spotted an interesting pile of rather smelly seaweed that had been washed up onto the beach by the tide. Becky could see a line of it, all the way along the sand—seaweed, and shells, and even a piece of beautiful emerald green sea glass that she slipped into her pocket as a souvenir.

Alex was already splashing around in

the ocean, but Becky decided she needed some more time in the sun before taking a dip in the chilly water. She wondered if it might be too cold for Cooper, too. But Sam, their obedience class teacher, had told them that spaniels usually love water.

Cooper started to dig furiously, loving the way the sand spurted up between his paws. It was much quicker to dig here than in the flower beds at home. But it did go everywhere. He stopped mid-hole to shake the sand out of his whiskers, and let out an enormous sneeze. Next he dragged a big pile of seaweed into his hole and covered it back over, scooting the sand back through his paws. Then he sat down on it happily, looking very proud of himself.

Becky watched him, laughing. "Should we go and see the water now?" she asked him. "Look, Alex is paddling in it."

Cooper stood up and followed her down to the water's edge, where Alex was hopping in and out of the waves, whistling through his teeth at how cold it was.

Cooper watched interestedly, his tail wagging. He'd never seen so much water, and it moved! He backed away thoughtfully as the bubbly surf crept toward him, and then followed it back again, fascinated.

"Oh, look, Alex! He loves it!" Becky giggled.

The puppy crouched down, his paws stretched out in front of him, wondering

if he could catch this stuff. This time, when the creamy water began to draw back from his paws, he jumped after it, splashing himself and Becky with freezing cold water.

Becky laughed, and Cooper shook himself in surprise. He hadn't expected

that to happen. But he liked it!

When the next wave came, he didn't try to catch the water; he just jumped in and out of it, shaking his soaked ears and whining excitedly. Chasing the waves was almost as much fun as chasing squirrels!

Chapter Four

On that first afternoon of vacation, Becky and Alex had been so eager to get down to the beach that they'd hardly taken anything with them. But the next morning, the first real full day in Salt Point, they took everything: water toys, towels, shovels, snacks, blankets, and Alex's enormous inflatable alligator. They struggled down the path, laden

with all they could possibly need, and Mom and Dad followed them with folding chairs and a picnic lunch.

It was another beautiful sunny day, and Mom insisted on covering them with sunscreen as soon as they'd set up a base camp next to a large rock. She looked doubtfully at Cooper. "I guess he'll be all right. But if he starts to look hot, you must bring him back over here so he can lie down in the shade of the rocks."

"Okay, but he'll probably just splash in the ocean like he did yesterday," Becky pointed out. "That'll keep him nice and cool."

Cooper was already running up and down the water's edge, barking excitedly at seagulls, who shrieked back

angrily. One of them settled down to float on the greenish water, not very far out, and glared at him.

Cooper splashed into the ocean, so it came halfway up his short legs, and barked a challenge. But the seagull only bobbed up and down and kept on staring. Cooper took a few more steps in, shivering a little as the water came up to his chest.

Becky had been sitting rubbing sunscreen onto her arms and watching Alex, who was kicking a ball around further up the beach. But now she suddenly noticed that Cooper was in the water. She raced down to the edge of the ocean, but Dad was there already.

"It's okay, Becks. Lots of dogs are

good swimmers. We can't let him go out too far, but don't scare him now. We don't want him to think that the water is something to be afraid of."

Becky frowned. Actually, she thought maybe they did. What if Cooper got swept away by a big wave? And that seagull looked like it wanted puppy for breakfast. It was staring at Cooper with its tiny yellow eyes.

Cooper looked around, happy to see Becky so close, and then took another step forward. Strangely, though, his paws didn't seem to find any ground to step on, and all of a sudden he was swimming, doggy-paddling as though he'd been doing it forever. Rather surprised at himself, he paddled around in a little circle, almost forgetting

about the seagull.

"He's swimming! He's swimming!" Becky yelled. "Cooper can swim! Dad, look!"

The seagull flapped its powerful wings and fluttered away with loud, frightened squawks, and Cooper barked at it.

"Sorry, Cooper!" Becky splashed into the water. "I forgot you were chasing him. You're such a clever boy! How did you learn to swim? Come on!" She dog-paddled along with him, even though she was in such shallow water that her knees kept hitting the sand. "Do you think he can swim a little further out, Dad?" she called.

Dad shook his head. "Maybe not yet—he might get tired quickly, like

he did with walks at first. Remember, he has never done it before. Just splash around in the shallow water with him."

Alex came running down the beach to join in, and they spent the next hour swimming out into the ocean and then back to the beach and letting the little waves carry them up onto the sand, while Cooper swam and splashed and barked delightedly around them.

They were worn out by lunchtime, so much so that Cooper went to sleep in the shade of the big rock after he'd eaten his dog biscuits and had a big drink of water. Alex and Becky lazed around reading while they digested their sandwiches— Mom said they had to wait for a while before going back in the water.

"It's been forever since lunch…," Alex moaned. "Can we go swimming again?"

"It's only been about 10 minutes!" Mom laughed, and Alex sighed.

"All right. I'm going to blow up my alligator." He lay down on the blanket and puffed fiercely, until the alligator was taller than he was. "Now can we go swimming?"

Mom looked at her watch. "Yes, I

suppose so. Oh, Cooper!"

Cooper had just woken up, and found an enormous green thing next to Alex, which definitely hadn't been there when he went to sleep. He raced over and barked at it madly, running around and around it, kicking sand on everybody.

"Ugh! Stop him!" Mom coughed, and Alex snatched the alligator up above his head, while Becky grabbed Cooper.

"Cooper, stop! Shhh! It's not a real one, silly. It's for swimming. Come on, Alex, let's show him. The water will wash the sand off us, too." She carried the squirming puppy down to the water's edge, and Alex launched the alligator into the waves.

"We'll have to be careful that Cooper

doesn't pop it with his claws," he said, holding the alligator steady.

Becky leaped on board and lay down. "You can tow us," she suggested, holding onto the side. "Come on, Cooper." She held out an arm, expecting the puppy to swim toward it, but instead he splashed into the water, paddled out to her, then scrambled up onto her back.

"You're a raft!" Alex yelled, and Becky giggled, trying not to wriggle too much and tip Cooper off. His claws tickled.

They swam up and down, taking turns on the alligator, and then pulled it up onto the beach and lay there on the sand, letting the tiny waves wash over their toes.

The sun was so hot, even when they were half in the water, that Becky almost fell asleep. She was just wondering how it was that the water seemed as warm as a bath now, when it had been freezing when she first dipped her toes in that morning, when Alex suddenly sat up and yelled. "Look! The alligator!"

She turned over and sat up. "What's the matter?"

"I wasn't watching. The tide must have come in," Alex groaned. "The waves have taken it out. I'll have to go

out and get it."

Becky stood up. "I can't even see it. Oh, no! Alex, you can't swim all the way out there."

The alligator was only a little green spot, about 100 feet from the shore, where they'd be out in water that was much too deep.

"Dad!" Alex called. But their dad still had all his clothes on, and even though he was heading over toward them, and Mom was standing on the blanket looking worried, neither of them looked like they were about to dive into the ocean.

"Dad, can I swim out and get the alligator?" Alex begged. But Dad shook his head.

"I'm really sorry, Alex. It's drifted too

far. You promised not to go into deep water, remember? Maybe someone in a boat will come by and pick it up for us."

Alex and Becky looked hopefully out over the water, but there were no boats around to go alligator-hunting, and the inflatable was bobbing further and further away.

Then Alex grabbed Becky's arm and pointed. A little golden head was suddenly bobbing through the dark-green water. Cooper could see the inflatable, and he knew that Alex wanted it back. He wasn't quite sure why Alex wasn't going to get it himself, but he knew he could help.

"Cooper, no!" Becky gasped. But Cooper was already way out into the

water, swimming along happily.

"He's too far out," Becky said worriedly. "What if he gets caught in a current and he's swept right out to sea?"

Alex nodded. "Let's swim out as far as we can—then we can help him back."

They swam as fast as they could, to where their toes were just touching the bottom. Mom and Dad were watching. Although Becky and Alex had promised them not to go too far out, secretly Becky knew that if Cooper started sinking, she'd follow him right out into the deep water. And she was sure Alex would do the same.

But they didn't need to. Slowly but surely, the alligator was bobbing back toward them, Cooper's sharp teeth gripping the white tow rope.

"Great job, Cooper! You rescued
my alligator!" Alex grabbed the rope,
too, and Becky hugged Cooper, who
snuggled wearily into her shoulder. It
had been a long swim, and his legs were
very tired. But he had done it! Becky
and Alex were happy, he could tell.

"Becks, get on the alligator with him,

and I'll pull you along," Alex suggested.

Becky nodded and heaved herself up onto the inflatable, carefully keeping Cooper's claws away from the plastic. Alex towed them back in, with Becky proudly holding Cooper in front of her.

Mom and Dad were waiting for them on the beach, smiling with relief.

"I can't believe what a good swimmer he is!" Mom said, scratching Cooper's wet ears.

"He's a champion," Alex said proudly. "We would have lost my alligator for sure if it hadn't been for Cooper."

Becky turned over in bed and yawned, and then giggled as a damp nose

was pressed into her ear. "Hello, Cooper! Is it time to get up?" She wriggled up in bed, and pulled open the curtains to look out the little window right next to the bunks.

"Oh!" Becky wrinkled her nose disappointedly. The sparkling blue water of the day before had disappeared. The sky was cloudy and the ocean had settled to a dull grayish brown—it didn't look like a day for sunbathing or swimming at all.

"Oh, well," Becky muttered. "It's okay, Cooper. Maybe we can go exploring along the cliffs instead."

She got out of bed and threw on jeans and a T-shirt. She could already hear Mom and Dad moving around downstairs, and she thought she could

smell toast. Cooper would need to go out into the tiny yard behind the cottage to relieve himself, too.

"Wake up, Alex," she called, tickling the foot that was dangling down over the edge of the top bunk as she went past.

Alex growled something, but his comforter humped up as if he were at least partly awake.

"Let's go and explore the cliffs this morning," Becky suggested a few minutes later, as she sat down at the table for breakfast. Cooper was already sitting hopefully by her foot, waiting for toast crusts.

But Alex shook his head grumpily. "No! I really want to go down to the beach at Salt Point. You said we could,

Dad! They've got rides on the pier there, and everything. I was talking to those boys we saw on the beach on our first day, and they said it's awesome there."

Becky frowned. "But we wouldn't be able to take Cooper! Salt Point Beach doesn't allow dogs in the summer, Mom said."

"Anyway, it's not very nice weather today," Mom put in. "It feels more like a day for walking along the cliffs than going to the beach. We'll do that another day, Alex."

Alex muttered something under his breath, but Mom managed to distract him by passing him chocolate-hazelnut spread for his toast, which was a vacation treat.

After breakfast, they set off along the path that led from the cottage, winding through the shrubs and prickly bushes along the top of the cliff. Cooper danced ahead, tugging on his extending leash, and winding himself in and out of the shrubs as he investigated all the interesting sandy holes.

"Let's take him off the leash," Becky suggested, after she'd unwound him from the bushes for the third time. "There's no one else up here."

But before Dad could answer, Cooper uttered a sharp little woof and looked around at her excitedly.

"What is it?" she asked, and then she gasped. "Oh, look! A rabbit!"

A small sandy-brown rabbit was peering back at them from the middle

of a bush. It looked terrified.

"Poor thing!" Becky whispered. "It's so scared. Cooper, you can't chase it!" But Cooper was already darting forward, the cord of his leash getting longer as he raced after the rabbit, which turned tail and dived down a nearby hole.

"Oh, Cooper!" Becky tried to pull him back, but he had his nose in the hole and was barking frantically. He'd been within a few feet of a real rabbit, and now it had disappeared! He could still smell it, but he couldn't see it. He dug and scratched, but he couldn't get any further in because the hole was too narrow. Eventually he gave up and slunk sadly back to Becky. For some reason she seemed angry, but he had no idea why.

"That rabbit was terrified! You shouldn't have chased it, Cooper!"

Alex snorted. "Come on, Becky! He's a dog! That's what dogs do! Spaniels were bred for hunting."

"But Cooper's a pet, not a hunting dog! What if he starts to like hunting

things and to chase cats?" Becky snapped back. "Then he'd be in real trouble. Imagine Mrs. Winter next door if he chased Jewel!" Jewel was Mrs. Winter's enormous fluffy Persian cat. Becky sighed, looking down at Cooper, who was watching her with confused eyes and slowly wagging his tail. "Oh, it isn't your fault, Cooper. I'm not really angry. It was such a cute rabbit, that's all."

"Anyway, that answers the question about letting him off the leash," Dad pointed out. "Have you noticed how close we are to the edge of the cliff?" He crouched down, pushing aside some clumps of yellow flowers to show the animal holes dotted around between them—and the little sandy

slope trailing down to the edge. "If a rabbit popped up in front of Cooper and ducked into one of those holes over there, he'd be over the side of the cliff before you could even call his name."

Becky shuddered. "I suppose you're right. Okay, we'll keep the leash on."

Cooper wandered on, sniffing hopefully for more rabbits, but they all seemed to have hidden themselves away. For the rest of the walk he had to make do with leaping at the butterflies, lots of tiny little blue ones, which kept flying around his nose.

Chapter Five

The next couple of days were sunny again, and the family spent them on the beach. Cooper and the children were in and out of the ocean most of the time because it was so hot out and the only way to cool down.

The group of boys who'd been on the beach before were back again on Wednesday, playing soccer, and Alex

watched them hopefully for a while, before the ball happened to come past him. He kicked it back expertly, and they invited him to come and join in. Becky didn't mind being left on her own with Cooper, Mom, and Dad. It was much too hot for soccer, and it was fun reading her book with Cooper snoozing next to her in the sun.

"Mom! Dad! Josh and Liam's dad is taking them to Salt Point Beach this afternoon, and they asked if I want to go, too. Can I? And can I take my vacation money for the rides?"

Dad got up and went to talk to Josh and Liam's dad.

"What about you, Becky?" Mom asked. "Dad and I could take you, if you wanted to go over to Salt Point."

Becky looked thoughtful, but then she shook her head. "Actually, I'd rather stay here, Mom." She didn't like going on rides, and she was really enjoying spending her vacation time with Cooper.

Alex went off with the other boys after lunch, and Becky set off on a long walk up the beach with Cooper. She hunted for shells and sea glass, and Cooper found a dead fish. He was upset when Becky threw it back into the ocean and wouldn't let him fetch it. It had smelled delicious.

On Thursday morning, Becky and Alex were hoping to go to the beach again, but Mom pointed out that they really needed to go grocery shopping.

"Do we have to come?" Alex groaned.

"Well, you can't go to the beach by yourselves." Mom shook her head. "Dad or I need to be there if you're going in the ocean."

"We could just stay out of the water," Becky suggested. But then she shook her head. "Actually, I don't see how we'd explain to Cooper that he couldn't go swimming. It probably isn't a very good idea."

"What about a walk, though?" Alex asked. "You did say before we came that we'd be allowed to go out on our own and we haven't yet."

"Yes, and Cooper really needs a walk, too," Becky added, exchanging an excited glance with Alex.

Mom and Dad looked thoughtfully at each other. "I suppose you could,"

Dad said slowly. "We won't be more than a couple of hours. As long as you take one of our cell phones, and you promise not to do anything silly."

"Great!" Alex cheered, and Becky reached under the table to pet Cooper. She could hardly wait for them to take their puppy out on their own for the first time ever.

After breakfast, Alex tucked Mom's cell phone safely away in the pocket of his shorts, and he and Becky filled a little bag with sunscreen, snacks, dog treats, water, and Cooper's special folding dog bowl. It was so hot that he was going to need a drink for sure.

It felt like a real adventure, setting off on their own with Cooper, and they were determined to make it a

really long walk.

"We could go all the way around the top of the bay," Alex suggested, as he hurried along holding Cooper's leash. "The cliffs over toward Salt Point looked really interesting from the beach. There might be caves and things in them. And we could look for fossils!"

But by the time they'd fought their way through the prickly bushes as far as they'd gone on that first cliff-top walk, Becky and Alex were so hot that they decided to stop for a break. Becky filled up Cooper's bowl, and he drank greedily. He'd walked more than twice as far as Becky and Alex, as he kept running backward and forward. He lay there in the cool shade of the ferns, occasionally snapping lazily at dragonflies as they zipped past. Alex sat on the leash, just in case, but it didn't look as though Cooper wanted to run off anyway.

"My turn to take Cooper now," Becky said, as she packed his bowl away in the bag and got up. "You can carry the bag."

Alex scowled. "Why should you always get to hold his leash? I'm taking him for this walk. You had him all yesterday afternoon!"

"What? For the whole walk? That isn't fair!" Becky yelled. "I only had him yesterday because you wanted to go to Salt Point! You didn't care about Cooper then, did you?"

Cooper looked up and whined worriedly.

"Oh, it's okay, Cooper … don't be scared." She turned to her brother. "Now look!" she hissed. "You're upsetting Cooper!"

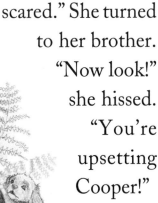

"I'm not the one arguing!" Alex spat back in a whisper. "Just let me hold him! This walk was my idea, remember?"

"No! It's my turn!"

Cooper whined again, but they weren't listening. He backed away, the leash pulling out behind him, and his tail held close against his legs. He didn't want to be near them when they shouted at each other. It scared him. He'd go and find somewhere safe to hide until they stopped, he decided. He headed a little further down the path. His extending leash was very long, so he could get a good distance away from the loud voices. The delicious smells in the undergrowth soon distracted him from the squabble he'd left behind, and he nosed around the bushes, sure he

could smell a rabbit somewhere near.

There was no rabbit to be found, but there was a huge butterfly—a brown one that swooped temptingly right in front of his nose. He barked happily and chased after it as it fluttered away. He'd never actually caught one before, but he was so close to this one that surely it couldn't get away. He ran on, barking excitedly and snapping at the butterfly, sure that Becky and Alex would be happy if he finally caught one.

Just then, Becky grabbed at the leash, yanking it away from Alex. As she reached for the leash's bulky plastic handle, she lost her balance, and the handle slipped out of her hands. She dived after it, and so did Alex—but it was too late. They watched the leash

sliding away as Cooper raced after the butterfly.

"Cooper!" Becky yelled, scrambling after the leash as it disappeared down the path. She could just see Cooper's golden tail, wagging excitedly as he chased after something up ahead. Becky took off after him—just as Cooper made one last desperate lunge after the butterfly, and tumbled over the side of the cliff, his leash bouncing uselessly behind him.

Chapter Six

Cooper scratched and scrambled down the steep slope, trying frantically to stop himself by clawing at the reddish side of the cliff as he fell. Sharper rocks were sticking out of the sandy earth every so often, and he whimpered as one of his paws caught against a particularly large stone.

At last, he landed on a tiny ledge,

about 15 feet down the side of the cliff. He sat there cowering and shivering, holding up his bleeding paw and howling with fright. What had happened? All he had done was follow the butterfly! It had disappeared, and the path had gone with it. Where were Becky and Alex? He wanted Becky to take care of his paw and pet him, and get him out of this horrible place.

"Cooper!" Becky screamed, racing along the path to the spot where he'd disappeared, with Alex dashing after her. "Where is he?" She flung herself down at the edge of the cliff to peer over and suddenly felt sick, her head swimming as she looked at the ocean so far below. When they were on the beach, the cliffs had looked so pretty,

pinkish-red with sandy streaks, but now they seemed menacing and sinister, and very, very tall. The ocean was right in at the bottom now, frothing and rushing around in clouds of bubbles and foam. Even though Cooper was a good swimmer, she didn't see how he could have survived such a terrible fall.

"Can you see him?" Alex asked, his voice quiet and miserable. Becky shook her head. "No. He must be—under the water...," she said, her voice choked with tears.

But then there was a pitiful wail from below, and Becky gasped. "Alex, look! He's there, he's there!"

She pointed to a tiny ledge below, where a clump of bushes and straggly

bits of grass had somehow managed to find some soil to grow in. It was just above the tumble of rocks rising out of the water at the base of the cliff. Sitting there, staring up at them mournfully, was Cooper.

"Cooper, stay! We'll come and get you—or—or something…." Becky's voice trailed away.

"He's all right. He's actually okay…," Alex whispered, gripping tightly onto two handfuls of grass, and leaning as far as he possibly could without going over, too. "I can't believe he managed to fall down there and still be okay."

Becky gulped, and tears welled up in her eyes. Alex put his arm around her. They were both shaking.

"He's moving, definitely. But I think he hurt his paw. It's so hard to see," Becky muttered. "I shouldn't have tried to grab the leash from you. I'm really sorry." She stared down at Cooper. "How are we going to get him back? It's such a long way down to that ledge."

Alex looked worriedly at Cooper. "I think you're right. He's holding his paw in a funny way. There's no way he'll be able to climb back up here! I wonder if I can scramble down to him."

Becky grabbed his arm tightly. "Are you crazy? Look how steep it is! You'll fall!"

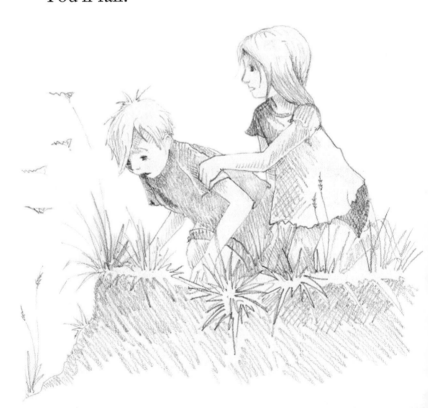

Alex shook his head. "Look over there—it's almost like a path, down to where Cooper is."

"Well, I can't see it," Becky said stubbornly. She could kind of see, but it didn't look like much of a path, and she was scared that Alex was going to fall, too. It was only a very thin ledge, weaving its way toward the bigger ledge that Cooper was on.

Cooper howled again, and Becky called down to him. "It's okay, Cooper! Don't be scared!" She looked back up at Alex. "Are you sure you can get down there?"

Alex shrugged. "No. But I want to try. It was my fault, too, that this happened." He went over to the little break in the cliff edge where

the tiny path started and gazed at it, chewing his lip. "I'll sit and wriggle along, I think." He edged himself down, very slowly, and Becky watched, her heart racing.

Cooper stared up from his ledge and wagged his tail hopefully. Alex was coming to get him! He stood up, wincing as he tried to put his hurt paw on the ground, and then he had to flop down again. There was definitely something wrong with his leg.

He could see Becky, too, just her face, peering over the edge of the cliff, so very far away. Cooper let out a miserable howl. He wanted to be back up there with her!

"It's okay, Cooper, shhh!" Becky called out, trying to make her voice

calm and comforting. Their obedience class teacher had said that voices were really important. If she sounded scared and upset, Cooper would be scared, too. She had to keep him calm. He always listened best to her in obedience classes; Alex got him too excited. Now it was more important than ever to keep Cooper calm. The little ledge he was on was so narrow. If Cooper got frightened and scrambled around, he could easily fall into that treacherous-looking ocean. And with an injured leg, he might not be able to swim.

Becky watched nervously as Alex inched down the path toward Cooper. He was going as slowly and carefully as he could, but the path was very steep.

Suddenly, Becky gasped as Alex's feet went out from under him, and he slid down in a rattle of sand and tiny pebbles. She caught her breath, jamming her knuckles into her mouth to keep herself from crying out.

Alex yelled in panic, and grabbed onto a bush, hanging on even though it scratched his hands.

"Alex!" Becky called down. "Are you all right? You have to come back up. It isn't safe. We'll call Mom and Dad."

Alex nodded. "I'm sorry, Cooper," he called down sadly. "We're going to get help, I promise." He dragged himself back up, going hand over hand and holding onto the scrubby plants that lined the path.

Becky grabbed him as soon as he

got near the top. "We should have called Mom and Dad right away. Are you okay?"

Alex nodded. "Just a little scratched." He showed her his hands. "But it was really scary. Poor Cooper. He fell a lot farther down than I did." He reached into his pocket for the phone and pressed the menu button to bring the screen on.

Nothing happened.

Becky and Alex stared at it in horror. "Try again!" Becky said hopefully, but the phone remained stubbornly lifeless.

"I must have hit it on something when I fell. Mom's going to be furious…," Alex muttered.

"That doesn't matter now. What are we going to do?" Becky looked around,

hoping that there might be somebody else walking along the cliff top. But they were all alone.

"I'll have to run back down to the road—there's a pay phone, isn't there? I have some money left from yesterday. You stay here with Cooper. You really need to keep him calm; you're good

at that. We don't want him trying to climb up and falling even farther." Alex frowned. "Becks, I can't remember Dad's cell phone number, can you?"

Becky shook her head miserably. "No. But it doesn't matter," she added suddenly. "Dad wouldn't be able to get down the cliff, either. It's just too dangerous. You'll have to call the Coast Guard."

Alex nodded nervously. He'd never made an emergency call before—but this was definitely an emergency.

Chapter Seven

Becky watched as Alex raced off down the path, leaving her all alone on the cliff top, with only the seagulls shrieking around her. Then she leaned over the edge again, digging her toes into the sandy earth so that she felt safer wriggling out a couple more inches over the edge. She felt dizzy staring down at the water, which seemed to be crashing

against the cliffs harder and harder every time she looked.

Cooper was curled up in a little ball now, with his nose tucked in next to his tail. He looked so tiny that Becky wanted to cry.

"Cooper!" she called down to him.

Cooper glanced up and barked delightedly. He'd thought that Becky and Alex had left him here alone. He had no idea how he was ever going to get back up the cliff. He'd looked down at the water on the rocks below, and wondered if he should jump in and swim until he found the beach, but the water looked very different from the ocean he'd swum in before. His little ledge was just above the waves, which kept rolling in and sending cold spray

up at him. And the rocks looked slippery and scary. His paw hurt, too, and he wasn't sure he'd even be able to swim. He'd pressed himself back against the cliff wall instead and curled into a ball, whimpering sadly to himself, wishing someone were there to help him. And then he'd heard Becky!

Maybe he could climb back up to her! The ledge was very thin, and it trailed off into a tiny little path that went winding up the cliff. Becky wasn't really all that far away, Cooper thought, staring up at her white and anxious face. He limped along to where the ledge got smaller and looked thoughtfully up at the path. It was very narrow. He started off up it, squeezing himself as close as he could to the side

of the cliff and feeling the sand trickle down into his fur.

"Cooper, stay!" Becky was calling to him. She sounded worried—angry, almost. He was only trying to reach her. Why was she angry? But he knew what "stay" meant from his obedience classes. He had to do as he was told, even though he really didn't want to. He sat down on the path, his ears drooping, feeling confused.

"It's okay, Cooper. I'm sorry. I'm so sorry…." Up on the cliff, Becky took a deep breath and tried not to feel scared. It just felt like Alex had been gone for such a long time. Every time she looked down, Cooper's little ledge seemed to have grown even narrower, and the ocean wilder. And if the tide

came up much more, the ledge would be underwater! She tried to remember when high tide had been the day before, but her mind felt foggy.

"Good boy, Cooper. Stay! What a good boy! Lots of biscuits soon. Stay! That's it." *Just don't move, Cooper, please!* she added silently to herself.

"Becky! Becky!"

Cooper looked up, his tail wagging. Alex had come back, too! He tried to bark happily to show Alex he was happy to see him, but jumping around hurt his paw, and his balance seemed all wrong. He slid backward, scratching and yelping, and Becky and Alex's faces appeared over the edge of the cliff, both looking horrified.

"Cooper, stay still!" Alex yelled. His voice was sharp and fierce, and it made Cooper feel scared. He skittered around on the ledge anxiously.

"Down, Cooper! Down! Stay!" That was Becky again. She didn't sound scared like Alex, but she sounded very firm. Not angry, but he could tell that he had to do as she said or she would

be. Cooper lay down flat on the ledge, feeling the cold water splash over his back. He wanted to get away. He hated it down here! He howled and howled. But he kept still.

Up above Cooper on the cliff, Alex explained to Becky what was happening. "I got to the pay phone and called the Coast Guard. But I didn't know exactly where we were on the cliffs; I hope I told them the right place. I said it was just up from Beachview Cottage."

"Are they sending someone?" Becky asked anxiously.

"Yes, they said the boat will come out from the Salt Point harbor, and it won't take long at all. The lady on the phone said it might even get here before I did."

"Did she say to do anything else?"

Alex shook his head. "Just to come back and try to keep Cooper calm, and you're doing a great job of that. And we should watch for the boat and wave in case they can't see Cooper." He propped himself up on his elbows, staring out at the water. "That's not a Coast Guard boat, is it?" he asked, pointing to a small boat, far out on the waves.

Becky shook her head. "No, I think that's the ferry boat from Salt Point. Anyway, the Coast Guard boat won't be that far out, I bet. It'll come around the edge of the bay." She frowned down at Cooper on his ledge, and the nasty-looking rocks below him. "How are they going to get to him, Alex? They won't be able to get a boat close

up to those rocks, will they?"

"If it's the inflatable, they will. I saw it in the boat shed when I went to Salt Point Beach yesterday. It's made for going in and out of the rocks around the coast. Look, there are people on the cliffs—maybe they saw it being launched. Josh and Liam said people always go up there to watch when the Coast Guard boat goes out."

Becky nodded, watching the little crowd of people gathering along the cliffs above the beach. She could see they were chatting and pointing at Cooper. If it had been another dog, she would have been interested, too. Now it only made her feel sick.

"Becks, look! I can see it coming!"

The Coast Guard boat was roaring

around the far edge of the cliffs in a cloud of spray, and bouncing over the water toward them. It was small, and there were only three crew members, but it was very, very fast.

"I wish Mom and Dad were here," Becky said worriedly, as the little gray boat shot toward them. "Maybe they saw the boat being launched from Salt Point when they were shopping. Do you think they'd come back to see what was going on?"

"Maybe. They might even be in that crowd over there." Alex hugged her.

The boat was getting closer now, and they could see the Coast Guard men waving to them. They waved back and pointed down to Cooper.

Cooper could see the boat coming, too. It was very loud, and he didn't like it at all. He barked at it, wishing it would go away.

"Shhh, Cooper, it's okay!" Becky called down. "I think he's scared of the boat. Cooper, stay!"

The Coast Guard boat had stopped by the rocks, and one of the men was climbing out. Becky held her breath anxiously. It looked so slippery.

"Hello up there!" the man called to Alex and Becky. "He looks pretty scared. Can you get him to stay? I don't want to scare him into jumping."

Becky nodded. "Cooper, stay there! Stay!"

Cooper stared wide-eyed at the man in the bright orange suit, with

his huge life jacket and orange helmet. He looked like some sort of strange creature, and he'd arrived in that huge noisy thing that was still grumbling and snorting below him. Cooper gave a loud series of barks, trying to sound big and scary. But the man didn't go away. He climbed slowly closer instead. Cooper looked around, desperate for a way to escape. There was only the little narrow path where he'd already slipped. But he didn't have a choice. He started to back away up it, still barking at the strange man.

"Cooper, no!" It was Becky, calling him from up above. "Stay! Cooper, stay!"

Cooper knew he should do as he was told, but he didn't want to stay! The strange man was coming after him!

"Stay, Cooper!" It was Becky's firmest voice. If he did as he was told, he might get dog treats—he knew Becky had them in her bag. And he was very hungry. The man was coming closer. Cooper stayed still, and looked imploringly up at Becky. Did he really have to stay?

"Yes, good boy, Cooper! Stay!" Becky sounded pleased with him.

The man was almost at his ledge now, and Cooper wanted to growl at him. He didn't look nice at all with that big orange helmet on. But he kept quiet. He was sure Becky wouldn't want him to growl.

"You're a good dog, aren't you?" the man called, as he climbed onto the ledge. The man's voice was actually nice, and

Cooper stopped shivering. "Look what I have." The man held out a piece of dog biscuit, and Cooper gulped it down gratefully. Maybe he wasn't so bad after all, even if he did look scary. "Want some more?" The man reached out and picked him up, and gave him a full biscuit this time. "Aren't you adorable? Come on." And he started back over the rocks to the boat, with Cooper tucked tightly under one arm.

Up on the top of the cliff, Becky hugged Alex tightly. "They've got him, they've got him! Cooper's really going to be okay!"

Chapter Eight

Alex hugged Becky back, laughing, and then turned back to peer over the edge. "Hey, wait! They're calling to us!"

"We'll take him around to the small beach in the boat!" one of the men shouted up to Alex and Becky. "We'll meet you there, okay? Are you both all right? Not hurt, are you?"

"We're fine! Thank you!" Alex yelled

back, and Becky called, "Good boy, Cooper!" They raced back along the top of the cliff as fast as they could, heading for the path down to the beach just in front of the cottage.

"I can see our car parked behind the cottage!" Alex yelled to Becky. "Mom and Dad are probably down on the beach. We would have run into them on the path if they'd come after us. They must have seen the boat and gone to watch."

They scrambled down the path and ran across the sand to the little group of people who had gathered to watch the Coast Guard boat pull in. It beached with a soft crunch of sand, and one of the men jumped over the side into the water, which only came halfway up his

big orange boots. Another of the men handed Cooper over the side to the first man, and Becky ran into the water to take him, even though she had her sneakers on.

Cooper was squeaking with delight at seeing Becky and Alex, and he wriggled madly, trying to get out of the man's arms to reach her.

"He's a wonderful little dog," the man told her as he handed Cooper over. "Take good care of him, okay? Don't let him go near the edge of any more cliffs."

"I won't," Becky said. "It was my fault that he fell. We'll be more careful, I promise." She laughed as Cooper licked her all over, and then licked Alex's face, too.

"You were right to call 911, though," the man told them. "Don't ever go climbing down those cliffs yourselves."

Alex shuddered. "We won't."

"Becky! Alex!"

Mom and Dad were making their way through the small crowd, looking horrified.

"What on earth happened?" Mom demanded.

"We're sorry, Mom…," they muttered. "There was an accident," Becky added.

"Cooper fell over the edge of the cliff."

"That cliff?" Dad gazed up at it, his face pale. "But we agreed you'd keep him on the leash up there." Dad looked from Becky to Alex. He seemed really disappointed.

"They did the right thing," the Coast Guard officer told Mom and Dad. "They called 911, and got us out to help."

Mom nodded. "Thank you so much."

Becky caught her arm. "Mom, can we explain later, please? Cooper hurt his leg when he fell; we have to take him to a vet."

"There's a vet on Salt Point High Street, just down from the supermarket," the Coast Guard officer told them. "Good luck. I hope it's nothing too

serious." And he splashed back to the boat, with everyone waving and cheering, and they sped away.

Cooper yawned sleepily and licked at the bandage on his paw. It was itchy, and he was sure if he nibbled it carefully he could pull it off.

"Hey, don't do that, Cooper." Becky sat down beside him, and tickled him under the chin. "You know if you keep chewing it, you'll have to wear that horrible collar thing, and you wouldn't like that. The vet says the bandage has to stay on for at least a week."

"He was so lucky not to break anything," Mom said. "Only four stitches, and some pulled muscles. It could have been so much worse." Mom's face was serious. After they'd gotten back from the vet the day before,

she and Dad had made Becky and Alex sit down and tell them exactly what had happened up on the cliff path. They'd felt awful as they explained that it was all their fault that Cooper had fallen and gotten hurt. Then Mom and Dad had told them how disappointed they were.

Becky shivered. "I know," she said. "I don't want to go along the cliff-top path ever again."

"Me neither," Alex agreed, munching on a slice of toast covered with chocolate-hazelnut spread.

"It's a shame not to go out, though," said Mom, getting up to look at the weather from the window. "It's such a beautiful day. You two could go down to the beach with Dad, if you'd like. I can stay and watch Cooper."

Becky shook her head and glanced at Alex to see that he was doing the same. "I'd rather stay here and be with Cooper," she explained. "Yesterday was so scary. I just want to be with him for a little while." She rubbed his ears lovingly, and Cooper yawned and nudged her with his little damp nose.

Alex came over and slipped Cooper a dog treat. Cooper gulped it down

happily. Everyone was being so nice to him!

Dad nodded. "Well, we still have three more days of vacation left. Cooper might be all right to go down to the beach tomorrow if we're careful. And it's good just having a quiet day, anyway."

There was a loud knock at the door, and Alex burst out laughing.

Dad sighed. "What did I say that for?" He got up and went to the front door, coming back with a dark-haired woman with a big camera hanging around her neck. "It seems you're famous, you two," Dad said, smiling. "This is Melissa from the local paper. She heard all about yesterday's adventure and wants a photo of you and Cooper."

"It's such a heartwarming story," the reporter explained. "And you called the Coast Guard yourselves? That was really good thinking."

Alex grinned proudly. "That was me. But it was actually Becky who kept Cooper safe the entire time that he was on the ledge. She was wonderful at

getting him to stay."

Becky smiled. "But it was our fault that Cooper fell," she added sadly. "We were arguing over who got to hold his leash and we dropped it, and he ran off and slipped over the edge of the cliff."

Melissa smiled. "I don't think I'll put that in. These things happen, don't they? I used to fight with my brother all the time. We'll just remind people to be extra careful when they're walking up on the cliffs." Cooper jumped down from the sofa and went to give Melissa a curious sniff. "And this is Cooper?" She patted Cooper, and he licked her fingers, making her laugh.

"He's a real sweetheart. And it sounds like he was lucky, too!"

Cooper barked happily. The lady was right—he was lucky. He knew that!

Becky beamed as they posed with Cooper for the newspaper photo—she and Alex on either side of their beautiful puppy. She knew he'd had an amazing escape. Becky rubbed Cooper's silky golden ears and smiled at the camera.

Right now, she felt like the luckiest girl ever.

Available now:

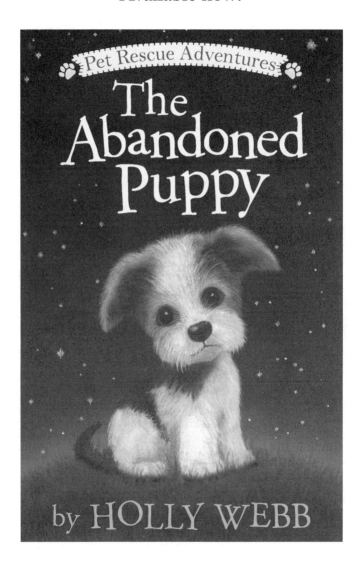

Pet Rescue Adventures

The
Abandoned
Puppy

by HOLLY WEBB

Pet Rescue Adventures

The Sad Puppy

by HOLLY WEBB

HOLLY WEBB

Holly Webb started out as a children's book editor, and wrote her first series for the publisher she worked for. She has been writing ever since, with more than 100 books to her name. Holly lives in England with her husband, three young sons, and several cats who are always nosing around when she is trying to type on her laptop.

For more information
about Holly Webb visit:

www.holly-webb.com
www.tigertalesbooks.com